The Topsy-Turvy Kingdom

THE TOPSY-TURVY KINGDOM

DOTTIE AND JOSH McDOWELL

WITH DAVID NATHAN WEISS

Illustrated by Lydia Taranovic

TYNDALE FOR KIDS

Library of Congress Cataloging-in-Publication Data

McDowell, Josh.
    The topsy-turvy kingdom / Josh D. and Dottie McDowell, with David Nathan
Weiss; illustrations by Lydia Taranovic.
       p.   cm.
    Summary: When the king goes off to war leaving Prince Herbie in charge, the
people become unruly and turn the kingdom topsy turvy so that up is down, cold is
hot, and right becomes wrong.
    ISBN 0-8423-7218-0 (hc : alk. paper)
    [1. Conduct of life—Fiction. 2. Princes—Fiction. 3. Stories in rhyme.]
I. McDowell, Dottie. II. Weiss, David Nathan. III. Taranovic, Lydia, ill. IV. Title.
PZ8.3.M46To 1996
[E]—dc20   96-18987

Printed in Mexico

02 01 00 99 98 97 96
7   6   5   4   3   2

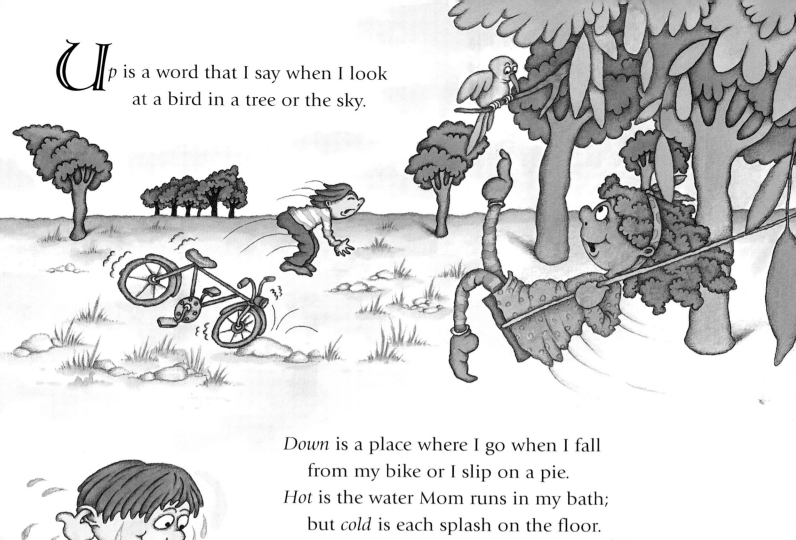

Up is a word that I say when I look
at a bird in a tree or the sky.

Down is a place where I go when I fall
from my bike or I slip on a pie.
Hot is the water Mom runs in my bath;
but *cold* is each splash on the floor.

These are all things that I know to be true
like I know two and two equals four.

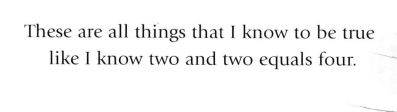

But what if the truth that you held in your heart
would suddenly vanish away?
What if *up* became *down*, and *cold* became *hot*,
and night was no different than day?

Now there once was a place in a time long ago
    where such a disaster occurred.
And as you might guess, when nothing is true,
    everything else is absurd.

People would walk on their hands to the park
   and bounce on their heads to the store.
Firemen only came out in the rain,
   and rich people begged from the poor.
It would have been fine if that's where it stopped;
   no cause would there be for alert.
But when lies became truth and right became wrong,
   someone was bound to get hurt.

This is the tale of Herbie, the prince,
   and his father, the king of the land.
Together they ruled over many a town
   and the woods and the sea and the sand.
The father was wise and was loved by most all.
   His kingdom abounded in joy.
For he had made laws to protect everyone—
   every cat, every girl, every boy.

The laws were quite simple, and everyone learned
to be honest and loving and kind.
Silly and fun had their place in the day,
but sensible things had their time.
Herbie enjoyed being prince of the land—
who could ask for anything more—

till the terrible day when the great trumpet sounded and called Herbie's father to war.

Of course, for a while, on everyone's heart
were thoughts and prayers for the king.
But as days turned to weeks, and weeks became years,
there happened a dangerous thing.
"It seems that our king has been gone a long time,"
somebody worried aloud.
"You don't suppose he was hurt in the war?"
Now a hush fell over the crowd.

P erhaps Herbie's dad will never return,"
a woman whispered in fear.

"I don't remember there being a king,"
yelled a foolish young man in the rear.

"Yippee! We're free!" said a silly old man.
  "Now we can do as we please!"
So he pulled out some pepper and sprinkled the crowd,
  and everyone started to sneeze.

Gesundheit," said Herbie, arriving from class.
"Why are the kids out of school?"
The crowd chanted loudly, "We haven't a king,
so now we can make our own rules."

Herbie was shocked and was sad and was hurt.
　(That's how his father would feel.)
He pinched his own cheek, and he tried to wake up;
　but it wasn't a dream—it was real.

I say it's best to walk on your hands,"
said a man with a very large purse.

"And I say it's best that *stop* should mean *go*,"
said a man with a tow cart and nurse.

And someone said, "Truth is always the best—
unless telling lies turns out better."

And some said that stealing from others is wrong,
except if you fancy their sweater.

Like warm peanut butter, this rottenness spread
till everyone took to the way
of doing whatever they liked when they wanted,
no matter what others might say.

Then, just when it seemed that all had been lost
and the whole world had gone topsy-turvy,
there sounded a blast from the tower above,
and there with the horn was Prince Herbie.

My father made laws to protect everyone—
    every cat, every girl, every boy.
And while we obeyed him and lived by his rules,
    our kingdom abounded in joy.
But look at us now—the place is a wreck.
    Oh, why should there be so much pain?
I beg you, return to the ways of the king,
    for living like this is insane!"

Then somebody hollered, "Hey, what's the idea,
    telling us what we should do?
Your father, the king, is nowhere in sight,
    and nobody wants to see you."

"Get him!" they shrieked. "No son of a king
    shall tell us what's wrong or what's right."
So they charged up the tower with every intent
    of launching the prince into flight.

Herbie slid down and leaped over a pig,
crawled under a Holstein or three,
then raced through the church and made quite a splash
with the ladies' group having their tea.

The Hand Walkers quickly began to give chase,
    and the Stoppers went *Go* all the way.
Those who liked stealing then brought up the rear,

and the Liars weren't there . . . so they say.

They caught up with Herbie, or Herb, as he's known,
  when he ran through a sign that meant stop.
And he was arrested and taken to jail
  by a fellow who wasn't a cop.

"Guilty as charged!" said the kangaroo judge.
"Your father, the king, is no more.
Mention him ever again and you'll find
you'll be leaving this place with a roar!"

People leaned forward to gaze at the boy.
Would he dare to speak of his dad?
Herbie felt dizzy and ready to faint.
Oh, he was too scared to be sad.

Finally Prince Herbie opened his mouth
and whispered so quiet and clear
that everyone heard every word that he said,
as though it were yelled in their ear.

My father made laws to protect everyone—
    every cat, every girl, every boy.
And while we obeyed him and lived by his rules,
    our kingdom abounded in joy.
The laws were quite simple, and everyone learned
    to be honest and do what is right—
even at moments like this one right now,
    when doing so fills you with fright."

Finally Prince Herbie opened his mouth
and whispered so quiet and clear
that everyone heard every word that he said,
as though it were yelled in their ear.

My father made laws to protect everyone—
    every cat, every girl, every boy.
And while we obeyed him and lived by his rules,
    our kingdom abounded in joy.
The laws were quite simple, and everyone learned
    to be honest and do what is right—
even at moments like this one right now,
    when doing so fills you with fright."

Enough!" cried the judge. "That's the end of the lad.
Now fling him clear off of the planet."

So all of the Flingers cranked back the great arm—
it took forty-two just to man it!

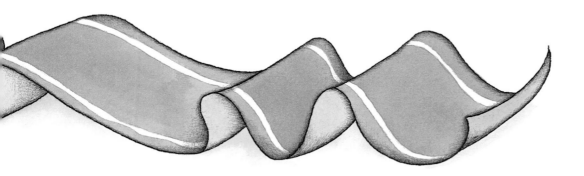

Then right when poor Herbie was set to be flung,
  there happened a very strange thing.
A powerful blast on the trumpet rang out,
  and the Flingers were stopped in mid-fling.

The people looked up to the tower and saw
  there clearly was nobody in it.
So they turned back to Herb, to blast him away,
  but a mighty voice roared, "JUST A MINUTE!

"I thought I made laws to protect everyone—
every cat, every girl, every boy.
But I see you've forgotten to follow my ways,
and my kingdom has lost all its joy."

The king had returned! And he scooped Herbie up
in a tender and powerful hug,
while all of the others tried sneaking back home
to hide themselves under a rug.

Then little by little they came out again
to ask for forgiveness, at least.
And the king was forgiving and gathered the folks
for a special community feast.

This is my son, who stood up for the truth,"
said the king of our hero, Prince Herbie.
"For he knew in my law there was power and love
to spare us from Topsy and Turvy.
So now, once a year, to help us recall
what happens when we go astray,
Herbie, my son, will climb up to the tower
and call us all back the right way."

So still to this day, in that faraway place,
the trumpet is played by Prince Herbie.
And I think that his people will never again
let their kingdom become topsy-turvy.

WHEN A KINGDOM

*Comments and questions
to help focus on the
meaning of this book*

WHAT IS "TOPSY-TURVY"?

Something is topsy-turvy when it is totally
different from the way you would expect it to
be. It might just be some silly little thing—
maybe a dog acts like a cat. Or it might be a very
serious thing—perhaps someone takes a neighbor's cat
home, pretending it is his.

- *When did something seem to be topsy-turvy at your house
  or in your neighborhood?*

AN ABUNDANCE OF JOY

- *What was the kingdom like when Herbie and his father
  ruled over the land together?*

Everyone was happy, full of joy. The people loved Herbie's father, the king. They knew he
was very wise. He had made good laws to protect everyone, including every cat, every girl,
every boy. The people learned to be honest and loving and kind.

FROM JOY TO INSANITY

- *When did the kingdom begin to change?*

When Herbie's father went to war and the
people changed his laws.

- *Did everything get seriously topsy-turvy
  right away?*

No, just silly.

- *What silly things happened?*

Someone sprinkled pepper on everyone; Hand Walkers
walked on their hands. It's OK to be silly—if the silly
things we do don't hurt anyone. But . . .

- *What happened next in the kingdom?*

People hurt one another. They made accidents
happen by changing stop signs to mean *go*. People
stole money that fell from the pockets of the Hand

BECOMES TOPSY-TURVY

Walkers. No one wanted to live by the king's rules. Everyone said right was wrong and wrong was right, so the kingdom became a wreck. When Prince Herbie told the people to do what was right, they tried to get rid of him.

TO THE RESCUE

• *When the king came back, what did he do?*

He rescued his son and gave him a hug. He forgave the people when they came to ask for his forgiveness. He gathered the people for a big party and gave a speech that turned Herbie into a hero because the young prince stood up for the truth.

• *What was the kingdom like at the end of the story and why?*

Everyone was happy again. The people were obeying the king's laws. They were doing what was right and true, so the kingdom was no longer topsy-turvy. Prince Herbie was there to help the people remember what happened when they went astray and to call them all back to the right way.

SOMETHING TO THINK ABOUT

Just as Herbie's father was the king of the land, God wants us to let him be the king of our life. Then he can show us how to live.

God is wise and loving. He gives us his rules to protect us. The bad news is that sometimes we disobey him by changing his rules to be the way we want them. When we do that, God feels sad. We hurt others, and we hurt ourselves. Everything becomes topsy-turvy. The good news is that we can ask God to help us obey his laws, which are found in the Bible. We can stand up for what is right. When we do that, we please God. We also make others happy, and we can keep our life—our kingdom—from becoming topsy-turvy.

Passing on the Truth to Our Next Generation

The "Right From Wrong" message, available in numerous formats, provides a blueprint for countering the culture and rebuilding the crumbling foundations of our families.

CD-ROM

Topsy-Turvy Paint and Learn CD-ROM
**by Dottie and Josh McDowell
and David Nathan Weiss**

This electronic coloring book is a companion to *The Topsy-Turvy Kingdom* picture book. Children can creatively color-in this unique and fun CD-ROM format while the "Right From Wrong" message is reinforced in their lives. Not available in bookstores. To order, call toll free: 800-552-2807

THE RIGHT FROM WRONG BOOK FOR ADULTS

Right From Wrong—What You Need to Know to Help Youth Make Right Choices
by Josh McDowell & Bob Hostetler

As the centerpiece of the "Right From Wrong" campaign, this life-changing book provides you with a biblical, yet practical, blueprint for passing on core Christian values to the next generation.

THE RIGHT FROM WRONG MUSICAL FOR CHILDREN

Truth Works! Musical
by Dennis and Nan Allen

The *Truth Works!* musical for children is based on the *Truth Works* workbook. As children perform this musical for their peers and families, it provides a unique opportunity to tell of the life-changing message of "Right From Wrong."

103 QUESTIONS BOOK FOR CHILDREN

103 Questions Children Ask about Right from Wrong
Introduction by Josh McDowell

"How does a person really know what is right or wrong?" "If lying is wrong, why did God let some people in the Bible tell lies?" "What is a conscience, and where does it come from?" These and 100 other questions are what kids ages 6–10 are asking. The *103 Questions* book equips parents to answer the tough questions kids ask about right from wrong and provides an easy-to-understand book a child will read and enjoy.

WORKBOOKS FOR CHILDREN

Truth Works—Making Right Choices
by Josh McDowell with Leader's Guide

Truth Works includes two workbooks, one for younger children, grades 1–3, the other for older children, grades 4–6. Each provides eight fun-filled group sessions. Through creative exercises and group activities, children learn four simple steps that will enable them to make right moral choices an everyday habit.

Contact your Christian supplier to help you obtain these "Right From Wrong" resources, and begin to make it right in your home, your church, and your community.